arrival

Also by Robert Nichols

Slow Newsreel of Man Riding Train*
(poetry, 1962)

Address to the Smaller Animals†
(poetry, with Lucia Vernarelli, 1976)

Red Shift: An Introduction to Nghsi-Altai†
(novel, with Peter Schumann, 1977)

*City Lights Books
†Penny Each Press

ROBERT NICHOLS

arrival

BOOK 1 *of*
Daily Lives in Nghsi-Altai

A New Directions Book

Arrival is the first book of the tetralogy DAILY LIVES IN NGHSI-ALTAI. I *Arrival.* II *Gahr City.* III *Harditts in Sawna.* IV *Exile.* The first two books have been scheduled for publication, respectively, for fall 1977 and spring 1978 by New Directions. The final volumes will appear in the near future.

Manufactured in the United States of America
First published as New Directions Paperbook 437 in 1977
Published simultaneously in Canada by McClelland & Stewart, Ltd.

Library of Congress Cataloging in Publication Data

Nichols, Robert, 1919-
    Daily lives in Nghsi-Altai.
    (A New Directions Book)
    CONTENTS: Book 1. Arrival.
    I. Title.
PZ4.N623Dai   [PS3527.I3237]   813'.5'4   77-1318
ISBN 0-8112-0653-X pbk.

New Directions Books are published for James Laughlin
by New Directions Publishing Corporation,
333 Sixth Avenue, New York 10014

To Grace

CONTENTS

ARRIVAL IN SAWNA

The rice terraces!

Blake, Alvarez, and Kerouac have just awakened. A veil has been drawn across the range of mountains at their backs. A squadron of geese coasts high up. From under clouds the rays of the pale sun slant onto the Nghsi-Altai landscape below, picking out clearly the specks of the villages distributed at intervals over the plain, and the shine of the Point Towns.

The helicopter has departed, bearing with it the crew of TV cameramen. Jack Kerouac is burdened with a hi-frequency transmitter which may be beamed to the United States. They have agreed not to make any reports for some days.

Alvarez rubs his eyes heavily against his coat sleeve, and Kerouac finds himself doing the same. All are dog-tired, exhaustion—or is it the altitude?—affecting them like a drug, which they are determined to shake off. They prepare to descend.

The distance from the ridge down to the Great Plain is almost a mile vertical. To traverse this the party has to descend by steps across the cultivated terraces, clambering down the steep banks which form the dikes, then striking across the strips of flooded earth. In these the sky is reflected. To the right, to the left, as far as the eye can see, run these luminous sky-mirroring terraces, a few yards at the narrowest, following the contour of the hills.

"We had better take off our shoes," Alvarez suggests. "We'll navigate more easily."

The thick oozy mud is up to their knees. Occasionally a plow team passes indifferently, both the plodding ox and the peasant bent down, intent only on the line of furrow traced in the water, and noticing them not at all. Evidently they are still invisible to them.

"Well—we've been invited here by the shamans," Blake says with a grunt. "When the time comes, I imagine they'll take the wraps off us."

1

Nightfall. Arrival at the first village, called Sawna. No square of "public space" within these Jat villages of Kansu-Hardan. However, a gong has sounded their approach, spreading out hollowly over the orchards and the outlying fields as they pass by, like some dye diffusing through the night. A crowd of villagers has gathered under a white wall, brightly lit by a street lamp around which insects buzz. They are led into the friendly glare by the shamans.

This evening there are only brief words of greeting by the elders and the presentation of flowers. The discoverers are allowed to retire early to the rest house, as the following day, the beginning of the Festival of Basora, promises to be a busy one.

THEIR LANGUAGE

This is how the official records are compiled in Nghsi-Altai. Writing is outlawed and has been for some centuries. However, computers are in general use for purposes of planning. All village panchayats, or common councils, have them, small consoles being set up among the hookah, or smoking, groups. In computer programing only the "stiff" language is permitted, composed largely of archaicisms and algebraic symbols; the common or "fresh" language is reserved for speech. (The above information furnished by the panchayat.)

Here is an example of a typical village computer-programed production plan, projected for the year 3670 for the village of Sawna in the Kansu-Hardan district:

Crops: dry season rotation (rabbi) pulse 50   hemp
              or cotton 80   millet 210 hectares
          wet season rotation (kharif)   sugar 120
            legumes 140   fallow 140 hectares

Industrial: cotton 1500 bales (T_c) light metals and
plastics 120 tons (M_{as})

(1) $\sum (PP(2000) + Q(130) + MG_o) = \dfrac{20510gk}{L4000}$

(2) $\dfrac{P_c - M_{as}}{\sqrt{T_c (L_{ca})}} = 1.00734$

> Where: PP, Q, MG are resource — productivity constants
> and gk and L are transformation functions. The second
> formula refers to a work input/population growth integral.
> It should be noted that the words "sugar," "hemp,"
> "cotton," etc. are in the archaic or "stiff" script and
> vary considerably from their equivalents in everyday use.

Kerouac wonders how he can use the above material in
his radio broadcast. He decides that he cannot. What he is
after is the "fresh" speech. The ear registers the color, the
flash of the spoken language. But how to convey this when
to reproduce it is illegal?

What follows is an example of the spoken language, a
story of an eleven-year-old girl, which the novelist was able
to tape. The tape remained hidden in his rucksack for some
time, and was later smuggled out of the country with the aid
of a shaman.

A YOUNG GIRL'S STORY

My name is Sathan. I'm eleven. I am waiting for my
husband to come. I have never seen him. I heard from my
aunt, yesterday, that my mother has selected him, and tied
the "red holding string" around his wrist, in the village of
Chadar Bhat.

How long will I have to wait until I touch him? It'll be
a year till I see him, at the wedding ceremony, then three

years after that when we perform Gaur together and he comes home with me to live in my village. In the meantime, I'll have to grow lots of black pubic hair.

In a month from now we'll have the first of the fifteen wedding ceremonies: Sagai. In this I shall send all of his brothers and sisters coconuts, his mother Venetian glass, and his father a pair of bast shoes. After my messenger has left, we'll all sit down and eat sweetmeats.

After that, let's see (counting the months on her fingers) —after that comes Balahdbat, when the engagement is announced, in his village, and in my village. On that day, hand marks will be made on the walls with red henna dye, from the gate of the village, all along the walls to my house. And from his village gate to his house.

He will have his hair handsomely cut, and the red nylon thread taken from his wrist and tied around his left ankle, and I will have my copper armbands struck off, and put on a necklace of jade beads. Then we'll both be given ceremonial oil baths, and rubbed until our skin glows. In his village, and in my village!

Once we went to Chadar Bhat. It was during Ghantal, on the way to the big fair at Garh. That was when we saw the shadow players. Chadar Bhat has groves of bay and almonds planted around it, and I guess beyond those, their millet fields merge with ours—somewhere. A monorail runs by there.

One day I was making chapati cakes in the courtyard of our house, with my cousins. Two of the American gypsy children came by, on their way to the well. They were carrying plastic buckets. "George," the freckled one, is fifteen, and his brother's nine. George was carrying two cocks.

"Won't you come with us to the well?"

"We can't go, because we're making chapati cakes, for tomorrow's supper."

"Come with us to the well. We'll go down the main street. We have grains of rice—we'll sell them to buy roasted rice candy."

"No, we can't go because we're making chapati cakes."

I looked down at my dusty feet and rubbed one toe over the other, and he screwed up his eyes. He held one of the white cocks over my head, pretending to be a shaman. The cock fluttered and closed one eye. He said:

"Someday you'll be married. But you won't stay here."

A prediction.

They say, "Tij comes and sows the seeds of festivals. Holi comes and takes away festivals in her shawl." Tomorrow Holi starts, and I have a shawl woven of scarlet thread, with red henna daisies hand-painted on it, which covers up my whole head. But in the crowd I can peek out of it, with my brilliant eyes.

Here in Nghsi-Altai men share the housework with the women and switch-roles. It is supposed to be same for field work. How I should love to drive a tractor. But the fields are all filled up, people say. "There are too many of us."

After the Deir Festival, the weather changes and food has to be taken out of the house and put back in the refrigerator. That's why we eat ice cream on Deir. The festival Devi-Ki-Karalis is dedicated to good marriages and keeping children healthy.

Kanagat is the time when ghosts come back, and also the time of the shamans' freak shows.

The festival of Siv Rati is to celebrate electricity and when people replaster houses.

And so the year passes...

A BOY'S STORY: THE FACTORY YEAR

Here is another story, a fifteen-year-old boy's:

In the old days boys used to do all kinds of real work in the fields. Now we're not allowed to. Now it is limited to tending cows, sheep sometimes. I'm in the fourth Age

Grade, but below that all you're allowed to do is play and take part in festivals. And that's boring. What I used to like to do best was swing swings from the high trees—and sometimes make double swings—and skip flat stones on the pond.

When a boy is fourteen he goes off to serve his factory apprentice year. I served mine last year at Garh. Some of the boys live in dormitories there, but most live in the apartment blocks with branches of their families. From the apartment block you can see the whole Drybeds section, all the way from one cliff to another.

I lived in our family's apartment, that is, my mother's relations. It's thirty stories high. They have no kitchen, only a hot plate and small refrigerator, and meals are sent up by dumbwaiter from the common kitchen. Also living there was my mother's brother's wife, who is my tatti, and their four children.

There are lots of steam trolleys in Garh. And almost as many chickens and ducks as we have at home. When my relatives came to visit me from Chadar Bhat, they brought poultry. People often have gardens on the roofs of the apartment blocks. One Jat even kept a cow up there. You see everything at Garh.

There are also lots of fairs: every week end, and also on certain festival days. Everybody from the region comes. There are girls from our own twenty-village cauga, or county. We apprentices were always following them, trying to guess who they were under their shawls.

My cousins were all brats, but my tatti was nice. It was pretty crowded in the apartment.

I liked going to work in the factory. For the apprentices, the classes run between five and seven a.m., after that there's breakfast. Then we do our factory apprenticeship until two. In the first couple of months the apprentices are taught chemistry, particularly about clay and glazes. Then we have machines for another three months, and learn how to wire generators, and all that. In the last six months you actually work in the kilns along with the regular workmen from the syndicate. The plant makes firebrick and ceramic insulators.

I enjoyed the electrical part the best. Though I'll probably never use any of it, because I'm going to be a farmer.

During harvest time, at Cait, of course everybody leaves the city to go back to help with the dry harvest, and the same way at Davana, for the wet harvest.

One weekend at Cait my uncle was away and I stayed behind with my tatti. She had complained she had a headache. That night I slept with her in my uncle's bed. When my uncle came back, he pretended to be very angry, but he wasn't really. That's the custom among us Jats, for a boy's first time with his auntie. When the kids were in bed, the three of us sat down at the table and ate initiation halvah. It's very sweet, and at the touch of your tongue it crumbles and dissolves into a sweet spit. With it you have a glass of peach brandy. That's why they say: "In the village it's black bread. But come to town to eat halvah."

THE GEOGRAPHY OF NGHSI-ALTAI

The discoverers have been given space of their own in the village resthouse, not spotlessly clean. William Blake, Santiago Alvarez the Cuban filmmaker, and the American novelist share a room with bunks. The sun in the morning, slanting under a latania palm, strikes a rose plaster wall.

What is one to make of this country which their travel researches have only identified as "the other"? Other Country, then. But how to approach it and experience it? The three keep closely in touch with In-tourist, the regional agency that runs this chain of travelers' resthouses. Blake and Alvarez have obtained some maps and a brief description of the geography of Altai.

Looking out over the nine territories. To the north, home of the Yang-shao, Lung-shan, and Jat tribes, lie the

Great Plains: featureless, almost treeless, a flat yellow-brown mat stretching to the mountain rim interrupted only by the gleam of an irrigation ditch, and the thin spikes of windmills. In the Jat section the villages are closely spaced, from one to one and a half miles apart, each with a population of three to four thousand. The ancient villages are sunk below the surface of the land for wind protection. The plains soil, fertile for farming though dry, is a tawny ocher most of the year. With the sudden advent of the monsoon when the moisture-laden winds sweep in from the east and from the Indian Ocean, the plateau is transformed overnight into a vivid green.

To the south of this lies the second biome. This is dense forest with a climate somewhat colder and more moist than the rest of the country. The Drune is sparsely populated. There are two tribes: the Mois, who make their living from silviculture, and the Deodars, or Bluefaces. Dwelling places are by the woodland lakes and consist of longhouses built on stilts over the water. Every opening in the forest has its settlement or cantonment around the lake, which shines at dusk like an eye in the prevailing dark green. Here the great ecological universities of the Deodars are located.

At the center lies the Rift, or Drybeds, bisecting the other two biomes. It is formed by a grand canyon and lies at a level some fifteen hundred feet below the plains. Entirely urbanized by the Karsts, this area runs in a sinuous line varying in width with the canyon walls, at the narrowest only a mile or two across, at the widest—fifteen miles. The base is desert with geologic formations typical of this sunken landscape: mesas, buttes, dolomites sculptured by wind; and also volcanic beaks, geysers, petrified forests, hot springs, and "paint pots." Among these, the mines and factories of the energetic Karsts have been constructed, and their linear cities under the bluffs.

Patterns of Nghsi-Altai. See the three biomes, its distinct landscapes of Rift, Great Plains, and Drune forest: a triad. And superimposed upon this another triad dividing it again, at right angles. Thus three autonomous regions are formed, each with the whole landscape. Each one having also the whole people, the Six Tribes.

Thus the pattern of Altai: a double triad. One superimposed over the other. A hexagram.

The areas are linked together by a transportation grid. Running from west to east through the brown fields are the irrigation canals. A barge is being pulled by a water buffalo led by a ragged child. It is carrying a load of sugar cane. Forty feet overhead, and rushing away at right angles to it in the direction of the Rift, the steel track of the monorail.

The Unity of Nghsi-Altai. As of a great bowl. On three sides the foothills of the Altai range, their flanks tamed into rice terraces. In the gray distances beyond, over a thousand miles of tundra and frozen steppe, lies Tibet. To the west and south the Indian upper provinces. And to the southeast the independent border state of Bhutan. Eastward of the hanging plateau, the dry bed of the Rift thins and flattens over a basalt ledge. The thin river of Nghsi slows, combed out by cypress roots, then disappears over the Great Falls. Nothing visible but the sky. The white mist, billowing and hovering, shreds and drifts downward over the Chinese province of Kwangtung.

MAKING A PIN

A number of old men not occupied as agriculturalists are the makers, or village craftsmen, of Sawna. One might say they occupy a privileged place in the sun. A wall shelters them from the wind; they sit on their haunches peacefully when not working, smoking their hookahs, yet enjoy the excitement of being at the center of things. The women of the village are always passing on their way to the well or communal freeze locker, or stop in to have some appliance repaired. A gang of children and dogs continually surrounds the old men, as their bazaar is next to the sweet shop.

In these sunken villages this craftsmen's bazaar is located at the bottom of a ramp leading down from the fields. These lie overhead, and extend out from the village on every side, devoted generally to vegetable plots and orchards. Beyond are the common fields. The village lies in a depression, scooped out of the soft red sandstone.

The travelers pay a visit to these old men. Blake, in particular, is interested in blacksmithing. They find this outdoor shop equipped with an excellent array of modern metalworking tools, including a small solar smelter. The stock, packaged in standard bar sizes, offers a wide range of alloys, all manufactured in the Rift. A nearby shop is equipped for woodworking and tinsmithing, and has a kiln for pottery making.

The art is demonstrated by one of the makers, a brusque fellow who has a harelip. A customer appears as the band stands talking to him. This is a Jat farmer who has come to have a ploughshare repaired. He stands at the edge of the field over their heads, halloos at Magor, and hurls down a piece of metal, which lands with a clatter at the blacksmith's feet.

It is the iron pin, or kus, which is used to secure the wood share of the plough to the curved wood handle.

"What am I supposed to do with this?" Magor holds up the bent kus, shaking his head in disgust, then passes it around to the other makers.

"Why, give it a few blows, you old fart."

"It's not worth fixing. We'll have to make you another. Just wait a bit."

And with this the farmer sits down, his back to a corn row, his legs dangling over the embankment, and begins to chew grass...

"Here, uncle, find me the right mold." While another of the old men does this, Magor goes to prepare the jig, first kicking aside a chicken.

The other makers continue to squat around their hookah pipes, listening to a transistor radio and exchanging insults

10

with Magor. Meanwhile the blacksmith has wheeled out from under a shed the solar furnace. This consists of an iron frame about the size of a barbeque grille, lined with small mirrors, the facets focusing the sun's rays. At the center is a crucible. Squinting, the harelip adjusts the focus and drops in one of the manufacturer's steel bars. In a short time the color of the bar lightens, turning first a dull mauve, then pink, then a blue flame pencils from it. From the crucible, the molten steel is poured into the ceramic mold. The maker shatters this after a few seconds. Holding it with a pair of tongs, he bangs the kus on an anvil to knock off the scale, then plunges it into a pail of water as the steam rises in clouds.

By this time the farmer has fallen asleep in his vegetable patch.

"No use waking him," Magor remarks. "Might as well wait a bit, and finish it up proper." The smelting process has taken only about ten minutes.

But now—as Blake, Alvarez, and Kerouac stand by watching—the work continues. The blacksmith devotes the next hour or so to elaborating his artifact, or as he says, "finishing it." This he does by reworking the back end of the kus (which sticks out beyond the shaft), reheating it in the flame, and hammering it. At the same time with the brazing torch he drops little copper beads on it until he has shaped it, very beautifully, into an ear of corn.

[FROM KEROUAC'S NOTEBOOK]

"Well, we begin by making a pin"—a witticism of Blake's. What is the next step?

Our Cuban filmmaker is worried about malaria. Before his siesta he climbs on his bunk on all fours and beats the corners of the net for mosquitoes. Is it mosquitoes they have here?

Magor talking to us the other day spoke of the holiday "Ghantal Deo"—has a nice ring. And perhaps we've celebrated it already. The other day Blake and I watched a color-ful procession pass by on its way to a market town, and the pilgrims stopped at the village pond to bathe ritually.

When I described this to Alvarez, he asked, how did we know they weren't washing their shirt?''

Blake and myself have become adepts at smoking the hookah: with some of the old men who were on hand to welcome us. Thus far we have followed no program. We are all dulled and wearied by the sights...the new sounds...

For instance: a bullock cart creaks over the cobbles, and the boy driving it is calling up to someone in a window...

We wonder how to proceed. I insist we shouldn't make schedules, and say to the others: "Let's just sit. Life passes before us.''

A COUNTY MACHINE BANK

The visitors, because of Alvarez' technical interests, have obtained permission to inspect one of the general-purpose machinery pools operated by the cauga, or county, and have left this nearby village of Dhabar Jat escorted by officials of the panchayat. A ramp leads up from the bazaar into a zone of private gardens and orchards (each extended family is al-lowed several hectares). Beyond this they come to the com-mon fields, where laborers are ploughing behind buffaloes. Alvarez asks the guides with surprise why there are no tractors.

"There were tractors in the old times. But a tractor is unproductive—not like an animal; it returns nothing to the soil by way of fertilizer. And in tractors the blade pulls too deep. It is not suitable for the soil here.''

"You mean you follow the so-called 'Japanese' system: labor-intensive and not capital-intensive?'' Alvarez asks. It is obvious the old farmer does not understand him.

"How many bushels do you get per hectare here?"

"Twenty-five hundred."

"That's not bad. Not at all bad," comments our Cuban expert in agronomy.

They come to an irrigation canal flanked by a bicycle path. A monorail truck appears overhead, stops briefly at a freight siding, then shoots off.

The machine banks, a regular feature of the plains counties, are protected by windbreaks of cottonwood, in front of which are several windmills. Beyond are buildings surrounded by huge piles of manure, some of them up to thirty feet high, of alternating dark and light bands, the tops sprouting weeds.

"Where does all this manure come from?" inquires Blake in astonishment.

They are informed by the guide that it is collected each night in the city, by a brigade known as the honey bucket men, and transported here where it is stockpiled. The manure is contracted for by the Farmers' Co-operative, which buys it from the city brigades at the exchange rate of one cubic yard manure to five sers of grain. The stockpiled material is analyzed by the laboratory, and chemical fertilizers and other nutrients added in accordance with local soil requirements.

Beside the manure piles is a large pond. It is rectangular and appears to have been dug artificially. Alvarez inquires if it is for recreation.

There was some difficulty in the translation of this word. "But what is recreation?" When it was finally understood, our guides roared with laughter.

"No. It is a solar pond."

"What do you mean, a solar pond?"

Incredulity that the discoverers do not know what these are. It is explained that the ponds are for the purpose of trapping solar radiation and are dug shallow and sealed with a black polyethylene liner. From the soil layer below this, heat is conducted through a series of exchangers to the bank's industrial plant, where it provides steam to the electric turbines. This is in the summer, the dry monsoon season.

During the rest of the year, the energy comes from the wind-mills.

As with many banks, this one is run by a Karst. The trio is introduced to the Karst manager. He takes them on a brief tour of inspection and explains the operation.

These banks service all co-operative heavy machinery used in the cauga. In addition, they serve most of the light industry needs. Unlike our own machine tools, these are not developed to make a single product only (thus being rendered obsolete when the product is no longer marketable). On the contrary, they consist of "banks" of highly adjustable, multi-purpose tools: presses, brakes, milling machines, etc. Of these the manager is very proud. He shows off, for instance, the drill for the extrusion dies, which is equipped with a photo-metric scanner and is adjustable from .0008 microns up to a diameter of 2 inches. Now this extraordinary tool is being set up to make aluminum irrigation pipe. The pipe is to be followed the next week by a run of electric wire and after that of lipstick tubes (a popular item among the Dhabar Jat women). This system is completely automated and computer-ized, equipped with a feedback scanner, and may be set up to make a number of runs, then switched over to another set of products, depending on the tastes of the regional consumer.

The tour ends. The visitors walk away slowly through the windbreak of poplars toward the village, assaulted by the twin smells of ammonia from the manure piles and of the heated plastic radiation liner. A strange combination.

•   •

It has been very hot. The house to which the explorers have been assigned is called a baithak, made of pakka or glazed brick. The walls absorb the daytime sun and give off a radiance. In the evenings—a welcome relief—the three sit out on their earth court, the light from the street obscured by banana leaves.

Santiago Alvarez sweats profusely. His ears are red. When he stands against the sun these appendages of his head flare, like translucent tomatoes.

14

Blake is listless, and the villagers marvel at his height—when he is not lying down. On the other hand Kerouac is all energy, a hard vigor. He plays soccer with the young men. They wear long trousers tied at the ankles and turbans. This gives the American an advantage over them, when lofting the ball with his head. And so he has become a specialist in lofting. He is much admired.

The pressure from the great numbers of people exhausts the explorers. They are not used to such numbers, crowding the lane on their way to market, filling Makers' Square.

Kerouac has made the acquaintance of some of the women—not easy in a country where the purdah shawl is worn. But the older women are less formal, and less cautious with strangers.

One of the families of the tholla, or neighborhood, has become friendly with the author. And so the party has received an invitation to dinner in a Jat household.

INSIDE A JAT HOUSEHOLD:
AN EYEWITNESS ACCOUNT

The children greet us at the gate. We are led through the dirt compound where a buffalo is tethered, up the steps to the house. In the kitchen we are taken before the matriarch. Saraswathi Bai Harditt is suffering from phlebitis and sits on her stool, her feet in a pan of water. In front of her is a two-way radio-television transmitter. One of the younger women is bathing her feet, head bent forward and long hair spread glossy over the back.

Our band kowtows before the matriarch self-consciously.

An older woman, the matriarch's sister, tells us that supper will be late. She explains that the fieldworkers have signaled in that a drag harrow has broken down. Saraswathi Bai has just dispatched one of the makers to fix it. It is this operation that the old lady has been attending to on the communications screen.

The talk which had died down when we entered is now resumed. Soon a girl sitting on a high stool recites in cadence. This is a worksong, so it turns out. The large common room is full of people doing a multiplicity of chores. There is a huge stove and food processing area in the center and a section of the room devoted to light machines. One group is making shoes, another busy with a mixer and roller. We are told they are manufacturing pills for the pharmacy.

Two young girls are playing on the floor with dolls. A boy sits against the wall. The floor is cold; his bare feet are tucked under a sheepskin. One of the young girls is Sathan. We are to see her fiance later.

"Hey, hey, where is Gerta?" The sister of the matriarch shouts boisterously. From behind others a small girl is produced and pushed forward by her mother. "Darling we have to have some milk. Do you think you can fetch it? Run now." The old woman claps her hands, and the child runs off into the courtyard, looking frightened. "And don't spill it!"

The matriarch's sister, a terrifying woman, is named Helvetia Harditt. She is about sixty and has a heavy black mustache. Again at her command, we are handed a glass of sendi wine and told to be comfortable.

"Don't stand around like sticks." This from one of the aunts. "And don't expect anything fancy, just ordinary fare, like the rest of us. We're poor people and can't afford wheat cakes every day." None of the younger women so much as look at us during this interchange.

Regular fare among the Jats consists chiefly of black grain millet or barley. This, fried and served with a vegetable curry, is called bajra roti. Another common seasoning is catni, made of onions, salt, and chili. With millet cakes people drink sit, made from buffalo or goat's milk.

16

By the stove, a cook in trousers stirs a huge frying pan of rice. Helpers are cutting up onions, the tears running down their cheeks.

Over the rest of the worktables heads are down and hands are flying.

Over a glass of sendi we converse with the aunties. We are told about the lam no custom of clan apprenticeship. Both young men and women are bound at an early age to work for these communal families. The service is harder for the men because of the practice of exogamy. A man must marry outside the village. He is working for his in-laws.

We suppose the burden lightens as the apprentices get older and they gain status by marrying and producing children.

Most of the housekeepers are women, but there are men standing by occupied with domestic tasks. We are told by the matriarchs that these are switch-roles.

As we talk, children run in and out. In this household they are served whenever they are hungry. The small ones are bare-bottomed, a smock just below the knee. The child holds out a grimy fist, and the mother or auntie, smiling, gives her a ghi cake.

In spite of the hard work all the Jats dress attractively. The standard dress, even for house chores, consists of a wide skirt (ghargki) spotted or striped in red, yellow, or white. There is the shirt (khurta) and the usual plaid shawl, obliged to be worn when there are men present. Then there are the low half-jackets worn by unmarried women, these often sparkling with rhinestones and little mirrors which are sewn in. Women also wear arm and ankle rings.

The switch-roles' clothes are more practical, though they have their own allure. They consist of baggy pyjamalike trousers (silva) and a long collarless blouse called a kamiz.

Suddenly the singsong story stops. A wail from outside brings some of the younger housekeepers to the window. They begin to laugh.

"What is it?" shouts Helvetia Harditt. "Now what's the matter?"

17

"It's Gerta, the one you sent with the pail. The buffalo won't let itself be milked. Instead it's pissing on her."

And now the fieldworkers have arrived. As is the custom among these plains people, they are served separately. The sober meal is taken in silence, there is no small talk. A housekeeper stands behind each agriculturalist's chair with a straw fan which she waves to brush away the flies.

At the end most of the family go out in the courtyard to play with the children. Later we all take coffee together, that is with the male members of the clan and the older women.

Generally by nine the men retire to their own baithaks.

I have been paying particular attention to the young women. From the time the men had arrived, we noticed, the heads of the younger women had been veiled in the deep shawls. It is not usual in this company for a husband and wife even to address each other, except in the third person.

Occasionally I try to catch the eye of the child bride, Sathan. She continues playing on the floor. The young man who is her fiance has recently arrived from another village. His name is Venu.

We are introduced to Nanda, Sathan's older married sister. Can there be some drama here? This union will make Sathan's husband her deva—a special relationship in Nghsi. Older sister and the prospective bridegroom talk easily together. They laugh often. Nanda leans over the young man, her hand resting on his shoulder. Sathan, still playing with her doll on the floor, glares at them both.

FIRST STRUCTURAL ANALYSIS AND
SELF-CRITICISM SESSION

The explorers have decided to hold periodic self-criticism sessions. Only Blake voices objections. What will it accomplish?

Alvarez reminds him they are on a voyage of discovery in South Central Asia. All three plan to send reports home to their separate sponsors in order to justify the trip, and each sponsor has his own expectation. Should they therefore not make an effort to co-ordinate the material? Disciplined self-criticism would serve to monitor the flow of information, evaluate its accuracy, and give a more balanced view.

"Bah! Balance!" is Blake's comment. Though he denies interest in "sending back any reports," he does not exclude the possibility of writing a poem or so at some future time.

The first session is held in their baithak. Blake sits smoking his pipe peacefully. Alvarez is cleaning his boots.

The novelist has adopted native dress, consisting of a tunic, or kamiz, and long baggy billowing white trousers fastened at the ankles. Kerouac's feet are bare. Recently he has taken to wearing a turban, but this is giving some problems. The difficulty is that the headpiece is not ready-made. It has to be wound around the wearer's head, and the band of cloth often gets tangled.

Before broadcasting the typescript of the foregoing visit, Kerouac has consented to submit it to his two colleagues.

The evening air is muggy. Mosquito netting drapes the windows.

Alvarez, scraping the mud from his heavy workboots, begins the discussion. There are many things about the piece he likes, that are skillfully done. But it tends to be superficial. The novelist has got the surface only.

Blake observes, "Yes. All those sights and smells."

"Naturally, an eye-witness account has to make it real. The scene has to be fresh, vivid," Kerouac explains.

"The buffalo pissing in the yard."

Kerouac picked up on this. "And the wail from Gerta. And the glare of the girl Sathan, directed at her sister."

Blake confessed he had seen no child bride at all playing on the floor with dolls or otherwise. "And is it necessary to deck them out in costume?"

The novelist said he was after a viva-voce description, some coloring was helpful.

"What you mean, I suppose," Alvarez said, "is Local Color. I see the tale is wound up with primitive and folklorist elements: the matriarchy, exogamous marriage, the custom of clan apprenticeship."

"What you are giving us in your proposed radio broadcast," Blake suggested, "is fictionalized anthropology."

The author confessed he had made some slight use of anthropology—a study on Jat customs in northern India—which had been one of his source books for the expedition.

Alvarez asked, "Isn't all anthropology a fiction—by the mere fact there is an observer, who represents an outside culture? What is observed becomes an artifact. And it is the interest of the anthropologist to preserve the artifact, to bottle it and serve it up to the sponsors of his expedition."

He added that there might be some uses for anthropology. "But we must identify the sources in order that we may be put on guard."

•   •

Kerouac has re-examined his "Inside a Jat Household" in the light of Blake's and the Cuban filmmaker's criticism. He feels he may be guilty of the charge: "fictionalizing anthropology." He concludes that he has done it out of vanity and to appear original.

He decides to make use of the sources all the same, properly identified. The book is Oscar Lewis and Victor Barnow's study *Village Life in Northern India,* published by Vintage in 1965.

But was it possible, as Alvarez had suggested, that this source might be tainted? The introduction to the work—which describes the village of Rampur—states that "the expedition was financed by the Ford Foundation, with the consulting anthropologists Oscar Lewis and Dr. O. C. Karin, head of 'Program Evolution' for the Indian Planning Commission—a department also financed by the Ford Foundation."

It is true that the stress is on the reactionary elements: traditional modes of behavior, caste relationships, etc. Probably one should be wary of this.

And to go deeper, one may well ask: who *are* these local students that helped the expedition collect much of its material? For instance the songs were collected by a G. A. Bansal, a graduate student and undoubtedly an Anglicized Indian. Doubtless his rendering of them, his translations, are not untainted either—being marred by certain "folkloristic attitudes"—and possibly a repressed sexual emphasis.

But can one say that the art itself is adulterated? The ballads do give important information. There stands the unadorned lyric, going back over thousands of years, and the naïve narrative and dramatic form, improvised by the performers to fit an occasion of the heart. One hears the authentic voice.

Beside these songs Kerouac decides to place his own poems and stories of Nghsi-Altai—in the spirit of frankness that Alvarez commends and in addition to give new factual information. Thus the listener to the proposed broadcast may compare the two versions as he likes and make his own evaluations.

BALLADS FROM THE MARRIAGE CYCLE

GIRL'S SONG: GOING AWAY FROM THE VILLAGE

(Sung on Bida: Sixteenth Ceremonial Step)

O Sathan!   you are going away!
My eyes are brimming with tears.
I would sew a shirt for my own Sathan.
I would place two lines of buttons on either side.

O Sathan!   you are going away!
My eyes are brimming with tears.
I would stitch a skirt for my own Sathan.
I would place two lines of lace on either side.

O Sathan!   you are going away!
My eyes are brimming with tears.
I would escort my Sathan to her palanquin.
I would send my brother along.

O Sathan!   you are going away!
My eyes are brimming with tears.
I will soon send for my Sathan
by sending her younger brother.

O Sathan!   you are going away!
My eyes are brimming with tears.

IN-LAWS

(Sung after Gaur: Twentieth Ceremonial Step)

O my friend!   My in-laws' house is a wretched place
My mother-in-law is a very bad woman.
She always struts about full of anger.

O my friend!   My in-laws' house is a wretched place.
My husband's elder brother is a very bad man.
He always slips off to the threshing at his hayrack.

O my friend!   My in-laws' house is a wretched place.
My husband's sister is a very bad girl.
She takes her doll and runs to her playmates, jeering at me.

O my friend! My in-laws' house is a wretched place.
My husband's younger brother is a very bad boy.
He takes his stick and slips off to the men's quarters,
   joking at me.

O my friend!   My in-laws' house is a wretched place.
The she-buffalo of that house is very bad.
When I milk it, it urinates, but when Father-in-law
   milks it, it gives milk...

SWING SONG

Daughter-in-law:

> Mother-in-law, the month of Savan has come.
> Get me strings of yellow thread for my swing.
> Mother-in-law the month of Savan has come.
> Get me a plank of sweet sandalwood.

Mother-in-law:

> Daughter-in-law, let it come let it come
> The plank and strings are ready at home.

Daughter-in-law:

> To others, your own, you have already given them.
> Before me you have placed corn to grind.
> I shall break the grindstone in eighteen pieces.
> I will spread this pisma [grain] throughout the bazaar
> Let the hali-pali people come
> Let them pick it up from the floor and eat it

Mother-in-law:

> Listen, son, how this foolish girl talks.

23

BRIDE'S COMPLAINT: A HUSBAND TOO YOUNG

There is a banana tree in the courtyard of my home.
I feed it milk and curd.
I go to my neighbor, sad at heart
My husband's sister knows the secret of my heart
She asks, "Why do you stand so sad and still?"
I say, "Your brother is young and still a babe.
He doesn't know the longing of my heart."
She says: "Take a bath and adorn yourself.
Make a wish from your heart and come with me.
I will make my brother meet you.
Even doors of stones would fall open
and iron bolts fall
Before your beauty, love and charm."

LONELY WOMAN

(Note: a love affair is permissible in this culture between the wife and her devar, husband's younger brother. Jeth is husband's older brother.)

O Mother-in-law, where should I sleep?
It is so cold.
My man has gone away to the army.
He is guardian of the country.
O Mother-in-law, where should I sleep?
It is so cold.
My devar is very young and innocent.
O Mother-in-law, where should I sleep?
It is so cold.
My jeth has gone to the fields.
He is the guardian of the fields.
O Mother-in-law, where should I sleep?
It is so cold.

UNTITLED

(Song about a rape [?] by the bride's jeth)

O sister's husband   I die of shame because of you.
My sister's husband said he would work at our plough.
and I was to bring him food to the fields.
O sister's husband, I die with shame because of you.

My sister's husband said that I should come quietly.
with no one seeing me.
I said that big thorns would prick my feet.
O sister's husband, I die with shame because of you.

They worked at the plough on one side.
The cattle grazed at the other side.
I was lain prostrate between two bullocks.
O sister's husband! I die with shame because of you.

I came home weeping and crying.
I told her my sister that her husband had brought about
        my death.
She asked what had happened, and whether I had been beaten
with plough wood or plough iron.
I said I had been beaten with neither.
O sister's husband, I die with shame because of you.

I was lain prostrate between the two bullocks.
They worked at the plough on either side.
The cattle grazed on the other side.
O sister's husband, I die with shame because of you.

KEROUAC'S SONGS AND STORIES
OF NGHSI-ALTAI

THE HOUSES OF SAWNA (1)

Kakka houses   of the poor   made of mud brick
Pakka houses   of the wealthy   made of baked brick
    fired and brilliantly glazed
All are jumbled together   there are no separate houses
The town anchors itself into the rock   Like a lichen
it has grown in layers   from the ground up   through
    the centuries

HOUSES OF SAWNA (2)

Staring at each other across the lane   the houses of Sawna
    form
two continuous planes at odd angles
      white stucco walls
   stained in the rain   henna   lime green   and ocher
A rough cobblestone street
   just wide enough to admit
a bullock cart   At the end of this story
   Sathan's youngest boy
Dhillon   will be driving it

HOUSES OF SAWNA (3)

I have said   that the Redwillow section
is a beehive of dwellings
Four communes or collections of families
      forming a tholla
these are the Harditt, Teka, Dhobi and Nai communes
under the leadership of the Harditts

As we approach
        over the great stretches of country
we can see nothing   only the windbreak
A cloud passes   the plain darkens for a moment
the heat shimmers

HOUSES OF SAWNA (4)

They are tunneled into the loess   the roofs baked
            a drainage ditch full of nettles
Swings hang from the trees
        left over from the Tij Festival
it is hot   hot   nothing travels but the clouds
From the gate
        a bridegroom sets out on a motorcycle
bells jangling from his cap

FACTORIES IN THE FIELDS

The grass moves to a sound
it is the footsteps of Rajpal and Harelip
as they go to the canning factory
through the tall grass

The stone moves to a sound
It's the factory manager   Tzu Tzu
            kicking a pebble out of his way
Can he kick a man like that?

On high grass
On stony baked road
Factories planted in the fields
        of the Yellow Sheaves Agricultural Commune
the brushes of the dynamo   go   wwhisssh   wwhisssh

I have made a necklace of grains of black millet
alternating with checkerberry
it is threaded over my heart

SATHAN'S SONG OF EVERYDAY CHORES

"Sathan   Sathan!
time to fetch water from the well."
The courtyard is dark   the streets are deserted
As I go carrying two pots on my head
the cold strikes through the folds of my dress
even the mirrors on my blouse shiver

"Sathan!   the laborers have to be brought lunch."
The path to the field is rocky and steep
in the heat   the oxcarts are drawn up
their backs gleaming   with sweat   the men of the commune
lean on their hoes   joking with one another

"Sathan, now the clothes. Laundry has to be scrubbed."
After work the village girls stand hip deep in the pond
the cotton of their ghargkis   sticks to their brown skin

A line of field laborers come through the grove
Sathan stands watching them
          soaping herself under the dress
one hand on her crotch   the other cupping her small breast

Oh my young flesh
my arms and legs   like sticks
My body
       Venu!   when will it grow
                 full and seductive as Nanda's?

NAMING OF PRODUCE

There are three categories of grains and vegetables in Nghsi-Altai, depending on use. Thus with tomatoes: those consumed by the commune for food, and also used for ceremonial and festival purposes are called frooz—a fresh speech word signifying sacred. Tomatoes allocated to the State Buying Co-operatives are called kijh—meaning tax tomatoes. The third category is kumbaj, meaning market tomato. Only the market tomatoes may be priced and sold.

The grading and sorting of produce is called naming. It is done by one of the village men's societies, the Squirrels. This operation is a privilege of the society, and appropriate regalia is worn. The Squirrels also serve as a special police force and give out fines to those caught selling sacred or tax vegetables. This is black marketeering and the crime is: mixing up names.

MATRIARCH'S SONG

Men are good for nothing
The young are good for nothing
Children and animals are practically no good

Without us   society would fall apart
The men would only make politics and smoke
The young paint their faces
          and dream of the next age-grade society
The children and animals wander around and piss

It takes an old woman to plan for the commune:
to run the data-processors   to buy grain
five years ahead   Everything harnessed and trussed up
the water squeezed from the socks
the veal pounded with mallets
the pie crust punched and rolled flat

Is it any wonder   we have hair
like wire growing out of our noses?

COUNTY WORKS PROJECT

The huge dam above the village
    rises higher and higher each day
Rubble and earth dike
People are toiling   hauling stone up in baskets
    winching up concrete blocks.

What a great Public Works!
Nothing to equal it since China in the eleventh century
When the great rice terraces were made
under Chou.

I am lying in a bank of huckleberry
    watching it grow.

A HARD DAY

    The herdsman marched head down. The wind had come up and he had gone back to the village to get his padded coat.

    The animals were not where he had left them. He spotted them at some distance over in the pasture that adjoined the Nai commune. The electric power line ran in that direction. He walked below and to the side of it, looking up at the steel trusses supported on the great pylons. Some of them were still covered with red turmeric paste where they had been "worshiped" during Siv Rati.

    The pasture was treeless. On the ground were the buffalo wallow holes, now empty. Ice was in some of them. Near the herd he tried to catch some of the calves, but they cantered away from him up on the slope, their hooves drumming.

    The cowherd made a fire and took his clarinette out of its felt bag. When his fingers were thawed he began to fool with it. The sound made him feel: What a pity! It's a hard life.

    Some Nai people came over the slope. They were men of his age, they herded for the clan owning the adjacent pasture.

With the music from the clarinette the weather seemed to grow lighter. They sat down with him and brewed tea on the exile's fire.

They talked of home.

SONG

Our eyes at water level
the woods reflected   green   green
          We have been
swimming through stalks of pond lilies
          New England
My daughter hangs on my neck
     while I try to write poems
          of Other Country

SONG

Venu the Bridegroom stops by the shrine
          on his motorcycle
I stick this waterlily in his cap

UNDER THE HARDITT LEADERSHIP

My name is Jagivan Sanjivaran Gopal Harditt
sixty years old   ganbu of the Red Willow Commune
          for twenty years
Come smoke a pipe with me and we will discuss facts

Beyond the lighted porch   there is a clump of banana fronds
At the edge of the smoking group
          dominated by graybeards
the young men stand   giving us black looks

They are muttering: how long will you rule?
they whisper: you made such and such mistakes:
for instance: why did you trade soap for salt?
why did you refuse
    to sell the commune's eighth part ownership
in the Nai waterbuffalo
    in exchange for a tractor?

Who is a revisionist? Who
is taking the "capitalist road"?

The street lamp comes on   and throws a purple glow
over the faces of these quarreling young men
    of the Kharab faction/   of the Dabas faction
I tell you the road's slippery
            an old man has to keep his wits
and stay five jumps ahead

MARKET DAY AT PUTH MAJRA

One day some of the clansmen were chosen to go to
market at Puth Majra. This the young men considered a
lucky break, a relief from village chores. The communes sell
their kumbaj produce at the seasonal markets, and several
members from each are assigned to transport it by truck
steamer.

When the Harditts arrived at the village Dri-Freeze, the
men of the Squirrel Society were grading and sorting vegetables. There were three huge piles of tomatoes. One of the
Squirrels was "Harelip." He was high up on the hydraulic
lift, balancing a long bamboo pole at the end of which was a
reed cup, or divider.

"So you're going to town today," Harelip shouted.

"That's right, today and tomorrow, we'll be there two
days."

"You're in luck."

The clansmen packed the kumbaj into circular woven reed baskets, called boats. It took six men to lift a boat. There were also boats of cabbages, chilis, and melons. These were loaded onto the steamer truck. The Harditts were joined by two Nais and three Singhs, then they were off to Puth Majra.

The road ran along the top of the canal dike. On the other side there were the commune fields. They passed a young wife on her way to take the laborers' lunch, a baby strapped to her back. The men on the road yelled at her. The Stanley truck steamer went off huff-puffing at a fast clip, blowing out steam from its rear and raising a cloud of red dust. They lost view of the village. Everyone was exhilarated.

"The old bus is really making time."

"Brother, don't run over that chicken."

They reached the market town in about an hour.

In Puth Majra, the government Buying Co-operative is located on the north end, along the flats. They dropped off one of the tomato boats, signed the papers, and drove on to the section of the town called Freemarket. As they approached the market the truck had to inch its way through a dense crowd of pedicabs, bicycles, and pedestrians.

"What a racket," one of the Singh men said. "And watch out for thieves."

"Look at them tall buildings!"

Inside, buyers crowded around the stalls. A wall of pumpkins gleamed beside a Jat truck. Pigeons wheeled. A barker shouted in front of a fortuneteller's booth. The thick air of the market was drenched by the smell of leather and kerosene. The stalls offered Drune medicines and liquors; Jat produce, melons, cabbages, pumpkins, and other vegetables brought by the trading communes, and cattle. Under a striped tent Karst factory representatives demonstrated harvesting machinery.

The crowd pushed against them on all sides. Along one side of the square they could see the large concrete building of the Conservation Ministry. The crowd surged, parted for a moment. A massed band of "Bluefaces," Sensor Cadets in green and gold braided uniforms, swept through playing a Sousa march, followed by a trained bear.

The Sawna men set up a booth and unloaded their produce. It was a hot day. The sun beat into the straw baskets. Flies buzzed in close. Some of the communards did the selling and keeping accounts. Others stood off unobtrusively in the crowd, to guard against thieves. The three Singhs were to be off duty the first day and "on the town." Toward the end of the afternoon, the best tomatoes had been sold. The rest were bruised from handling and being picked over. There would be enough for the next day, though the prices would drop.

The square began to empty. The stall next to them shut down. A loudspeaker from the Syndicate Hall announced a soccer match to be played that evening.

The three Singh men returned in high spirits. They had been shopping. One of them had bought a portable phonograph and records in the Foreign Quarter. After supper the villagers sent over to a restaurant for coffee, then they squatted together on the cobblestone pavement. One of the Singhs took coins from his pocket. He made four little piles on the ground, sorting the coins of the same sizes together. He squinted.

"Don't you understand money?" he was asked.

"He hasn't been to the city since his factory year," another Singh explained.

But the man liked to use it. He swept the coins together into his palms. He jingled them, and then smelled them. The others laughed.

"Tonight, man, we're going to have ourselves a time."

One of them said that they were going to Paradise—the American gypsy section.

One of the salesmen had begun to play his harmonica.

The square was relatively deserted now. An old lady with a shopping bag bent over the straw boat picking over the tomatoes, the rim against her waist. She was one of the poor Karsts. There would be more of them that evening.

34

A Nai took out his paint pot and began to decorate himself. Holding up a small mirror he drew sketches on his face carefully. He was followed by the others.

The decorations were geometrical: straight blue lines over the body, in fine arabesques, starting at the lips, dividing the face into quadrants. Some of the men had brought guitars and a bagpipe. The Sawna men played riffs back and forth. Then they turned on the phonograph and improvised along with it. The record was a Coleman Hawkins piece. They played against it, the instruments weaving in and out of it, now in counterpoint to the tune, now drifting along with it. So that people around them in the square waited or moved softly.

The square was empty and dark now. From a distance over the city roofs, an aura of lights and shouts beckoned them, but nobody paid any attention. The painted clansmen played softly, and all around them people sat listening wrapped in their blankets, or lay asleep under their booths on the stones... In the big city... on the great square of Puth Majra...

SECOND STRUCTURAL ANALYSIS AND SELF-CRITICISM: ALVAREZ' REPORT

Blake has taken up a musical instrument, the gusle. The trio first heard the native product at the Harditt household accompanying a dance during one of the festivals.

Blake plays but he does not sing. What words, what language, would he use? But he does chant and growl when practicing his gusle.

A friend from the Weather and Soils Station has been teaching him. Bomba, one of the so-called Blue Deodars.

Santiago Alvarez has become popular with the ganbus, leaders of the village production teams. They have given him a merit badge for his enthusiasm cutting sugar cane. In fact the Cuban is an outstanding filmmaker but a poor cane cutter. During the first weeks he suffered agony from blisters. Now he wears gloves when wielding the machete. But he vows that someday he will cut cane barehanded.

Tonight Blake has brought his Deodar friend to the bathaik—accompanied by the latter's tame puma. The two are inseparable. Blake, Bomba, and the puma sprawl on one of the bunks yawning.

Alvarez has invited several guests of his own. They are members of the panchayat, and seem to be the oldest and most doddering of these village notables. Alvarez' purpose is to enlarge the range of the group's "self-criticism." He will read his report on Sawna. By including some of the native population, he hopes to get a more comprehensive view.

Alvarez begins to read his report, but after a few minutes Bomba, the soils and weather technician, gets up to leave, excusing himself. The puma follows him.

Blake lingers on the porch with his friend. They converse softly, looking up at the sky. A warm wind has come from the east, which, they say, will "push the peach blossoms."

Alvarez resumes. The report, on the economics of Nghsi-Altai, is addressed to Alvarez' sponsor, a publishing organization.

To: The People's Voice
Cuban-American Friendship Society
9 Rockefeller Plaza, New York, N. Y.

This will be my first full-scale report. Recently I have been engaged in detailed discussions with the Regional Planning Office, Kansu-Hardan district. Their chief planner, a Mr. J. P. Naroyan, has been very helpful to me in going over the general picture. He has also suggested that I look into two of his own pamphlets, "Socialism to Sarvodoy," Madras, 1956 (written when he was with the Indian Congress Party), and "Village Republics: Swaraj for the People," Benares, 1961. Unfortunately neither is available in the U.S.

36

J.P., the chief planner, also gave me useful historical background (which has not been forthcoming from the shamans contacted by Blake, and is of course beyond the scope of Kerouac's glosses).

Alvarez paused in his reading to give a look of apology at his colleagues.

We are concerned with how this system (of political economy) works. And of course we must look for the answer through the method of dialectical materialism, i.e. in the modes of production and property relations which lie below the superstructure.

We must place our observations within the proper ideological framework. But at the outset I am puzzled. But which model are we to follow?

Marxist-Leninist?

The Frankfurt school?

Rosa Luxemburg?

Gramsci?

None of the orthodox models exactly fits. However, I *resist* going the road of anarchosyndicalism (Bakunin and Co. after their expulsion from First International).

Here is the preliminary scheme:

FIRST THESIS (FOR A DESCRIPTION OF NGHSI-ALTAI): MODES OF PRODUCTION DETERMINE HISTORICAL DEVELOPMENT

We Marxists understand the relation between technological development and fundamental property relations. The great technological inventions (wind, steam, water power) that came to Europe from the ninth to the twelfth centuries were grafted on the base of feudalism. This stage passed rapidly into capitalism producing its appropriate energy forms—an immense steel-coal aggregation organized around the nation-state. (And later petroleum and worldwide monopoly capitalism.)

In Nghsi-Altai this stage has been by-passed. Apparently, the Industrial Revolution came several centuries earlier. With no base for heavy capital-formation, the system has gone directly into an open, intermediate-scale technology. This technology is highly sophisticated. It is based not on extractive fuels, but on other free energy sources. These are wind, solar, and geothermal energy. Compared with our own, these are low-yield energy systems. They imply decentralization and must be tied in closely to a regional economy.

Possibly we must look for answers on a plane somewhere below state socialism and national planning. Unfortunately in Nghsi there is no State. I am loathe to descend to the level of regionalism, with its "populist" ideology. But again this is most emphatically *not* the regionalism of Godwin and Proudhon, the Italian anarchist Malatesta, Murray Bookchin, *et al.*

SECOND THESIS: NO URBAN-RURAL DICHOTOMY, UNIFIED SYSTEM VS. SATELLIZATION

In the West the rural economy has been satellized by the city, not only under capitalism but regrettably under socialism as well. However in the Nghsi-Altai the operating unit is the confederation (see the early Russian revolutionary soviets). The city itself has been broken up, so that its subdivisions (or sections) relate directly to the surrounding countryside in the same way as the Paris sections of the 1790s related to their rural departments, and relied on them for food supply. I am told there is virtually no central municipal administration. Naroyan suggests another example in our own day would be twentieth-century Calcutta, which is hardly a city at all but an agglomeration of practically self-governing birlahs, each with its own nationality groups and even its own language.

(Note: The above is clearly *not* Kropotkin's romanticized "countrification," *viz.* his *Conquest of Bread.* You will agree that my analysis of the failure of the Paris Commune differs from Kropotkin's radically.)

One can say that the city has been dis-urbanized. At the same time the countryside has been allowed to develop hegemony, through the means of its own production and industry sectors. For instance the market sector of Puth Majra produces tractors and railway carriages. Each county has its own light industry complex, the "machine banks."

THIRD THESIS: HIGH LABOR VALUE VS. CAPITAL RATIO

The key here is population differences between Asia and United States/Europe. Population density in Nghsi-Altai is at a maximum of 3,000-4,000 persons/sq. mi. (similar to present-day Ceylon; and at a level predicted for the West not until the year 2800). Under the circumstances one would not expect to find a value system which sets a premium on machines as labor-saving devices. On the contrary the Nghsi-Altai system maximizes labor power, i.e. it is labor- rather than capital-intensive. The only machines developed are those which increase productivity but do not penalize employment. There may be some exceptions here (telecommunications?).

Thus in Nghsi socialism has not "succeeded the last stage of capitalism," or been built on mature capitalist modes of production. In this country it has by-passed them. Does this mean that capitalism lies in the future here? Possibly.

I know of only one school of economics in the West which advocates smaller production units and denies the efficiencies of scale associated with both capitalism and communism. This is a minor tendency—the so-called Middle Technology Development Group, whose most noted proponent is E. F. Schumacher. See his *Small Is Beautiful, Buddhist Economics,* and other works of petty-bourgeois romanticism.

I am also disturbed that the authorities here have permitted a limited Free Market sector. Probably this is transitional—not a permanent feature (as the unfortunate aberration in Yugoslavia)."

The filmmaker had finished. He turned to the others. But the local notables had left—including it seems Naroyan himself, whose works the Cuban had alluded to. Blake had fallen asleep. Alvarez dropped his report heavily on the bed and asked Kerouac: "What do you think of it?"

"I really dig all your negations. That's an art form in itself."

• •

Blake has been absent from Sawna a good deal of the time.

Where has he been? He goes off cheerfully with his rucksack and walking stick into the landscape. Blake is detached from the explorer's party, and his mind is hardly engaged in the business of making reports.

On the other hand Blake is something of an embarrassment to Alvarez and Kerouac. They have found that he has made several trips to the Drune Forest in the company of Bomba. Possibly they have set up a hut there in the woods and are enjoying nature, with the puma.

But Blake returns at intervals. Then he is all affability. He goes to considerable trouble to keep abreast of Alvarez' researches. The progress of Kerouac's narrative interests him less.

THIRD SELF-CRITICISM SESSION:
BLAKE ON THE PLAYFUL

Blake in one of his rare good moods. In the past he has been unenthusiastic about the form "mutual self-criticism" (as being inappropriate to genius). However today he is willing to indulge his colleagues. Would they care to have his views?

"Yes. Let's get into it."

As for Kerouac, Blake suggests, the novelist has been following a tried and true literary formula: the subject presented as personal, and to some extent, sexual biography. "The ardors of the flesh have been spied upon...a tireless indexing of the body in all its modes" (the sage quotes from a well-known existentialist).

On the other hand Alvarez has given the material base, and by extension the social context. Blake feels that the approaches worked together. "No artist can convey the whole. But between you, you get the Nghsi-Altai character pretty well. But you have left out something essential."

They ask him what was that?

"It is simply: worship. The element of the marvelous. And the lives of the people of Altai are organically connected to it." Therefore Blake would prefer to recast their joint account. He would like to arrange it as a chronology of the various Year Festivals, the sacred holidays.

Alvarez' reaction: this would be "mere obscurantism."

"The obscure...the obscure," the poet muttered. "How do you suggest we penetrate the veil?"

Kerouac's difficulty with this approach: that it might be accurate but would be unbelievable to the folks back home. "We have a secular audience."

Blake: "But this country is permeated by the sacred. It's what gives it its aura. Not to take account of it in your exploration would be like going to the moon and bringing back only rocks."

"And that brings me to the next point: style. You'll pardon my saying so, but you are both too literal, each in your own way, and therefore somewhat mechanistic. The universe of the miraculous calls forth the mode of Play. One's style should be playful, vis-à-vis the reader or listener, and it should be obvious that one is playing."

Blake recommends a number of stylistic tricks: the fictional narrator, the plot within the plot, etc. As an example he offers Cervantes: this author was usually credited with giving the world Don Quixote, but in fact had assumed a whole gallery of disguises. He had interrupted his tale with pastoral romances, taken from who knows where, and insisted that a large part of the text was from an ancient Arabic manuscript written by the scribe Sid Hemmete Bennegeli.

"And now I'm going to tell you a story. I'm curious to know what you think of it."

Blake tells the following story, called "The Insect Pilgrimage," which he claims has been related to him by Bomba.

THE INSECT PILGRIMAGE: FIRST PART

After ten years of marriage it is traditional for couples in Nghsi-Altai to go on their "insect pilgrimage." It is called that because it is done in the wet month, Asauj, when the insects swarm in the fields. The pilgrimage is to the Drune, to one of the forest universities.

Venu and Sathan had departed from Sawna with their three children. They had left by monorail around noon and by five were in the Garh station in the Drybeds. They had spent the night at a cousin's apartment, in one of the quarters inhabited by Chandpur people. The next day they set out again, by trolley across town. At the base of the cliff they transferred to cable car.

As they approached the top of the cliff face, they could see the layers and striations of soil, could almost touch the birds' nests. They wore their ceremonial face and body ornaments. Their dress denoted that they were passing into another age group.

Below them, filling the grand canyon, lay the familiar city of Garh. They were at a level with the roofs of the point houses and the antennae of wireless stations. Across the flats was the great steel mill complex powered through its steam ducts. The chalk face of the cliff stood opposite them. Beyond they could see the beginning of the plains, and in the distance, the windmills that stood over their own familiar fields.

Here is the point, crucial in the life of every Nghsi-Altai citizen, where one says good-by to the old life and turns to the new, not without some pain. At the edge of the precipice, Venu took out a carton he had brought with him which contained the "four souls": bread, water, earth, and a sample in a bottle of the air of their native Sawna neighborhood. These he loosed into the Rift, for the Place Spirits. Then he and his wife turned. From a perforated locket around her neck, Sathan drew out a striped caterpillar. With a prayer she placed this on a forest leaf. Now it would go into its resting stage, and break from its chrysalis in a few weeks to become a monarch butterfly. This ceremony marked the start of their pilgrimage.

Beyond the canyon rim the Drune forest begins. For the first day the road ran in a cutting between the trees following a railroad bed. At intervals there are intersections of railroads, and trading settlements. Here one began to see the Mois. On the road also they met Thays, the children in furs bound on the travois sledges. As they passed, the Harditt children saluted them.

The last railroads had gone. After the small forest cantonment of Oodagoodooga, the road became a trail. The leaf cover of the great trees came together over their heads. But here the trees were primeval, and there were spaces in between every so often where the sun filtered through and there were flowers. It was their first trip away from the commune. At night they pitched camp, the children sleeping in a tent, and Sathan and Venu on the ground in a sleeping bag.

They had never made love to each other alone before. Venu had slept with other women in the fields. But with his clan wife, with Sathan when he had the urge, he had come to the common quarters from the men's club, found her among the sleeping forms, and made love to her briefly before orgasm.

Here they were alone under the sleeping leaves. Their sex play lasted a long time, and it was tender. The massiveness of her response excited him. They slept in each other's embrace. And in the morning when they awoke and looked into each other's eyes, the novelty of this struck them, they were almost ashamed.

The children brought them gifts from the woods. Maddi and Dhillon brought snails. Srikant, the oldest boy, was now six. Everything he found in the wood delighted him. He was up at dawn, and arrived each breakfast with a new kind of shining beetle or berry. They proceeded farther into the drune.

Gradually the ground ascended, and the hardwood forest gave way to conifers. They met fewer Thays and more Deodars on the trail. By the fifth day they had arrived at the Drune cantonment of Egwegnu.

At this point the narrator paused to fill the pipe with bang, a habit he had picked up from the shamans.

"What is Egwegnu?" Alvarez asked.

Blake replied: "It is a lake city, the seat of the great ecological university."

"And what is that?" Jack Kerouac asked. "The tale is fascinating—and improbable."

But the seer had had enough of storytelling for the evening. They relapsed into smoking their hookah. Blake and the novelist pulled alternately on the ivory stem attached through a long tube to the transparent chamber, and watched the water bubble.

AN ACCIDENT ON THE HIGHWAY

The travelers have learned of the death of Kerouac. This misfortune occurred several days after Blake's recounting of the second half of his "Insect Pilgrimage" story.

The event, totally unexpected, has cast a shadow over the expedition.

The two were informed by the authorities of the regional panchayat that their friend had been "the victim of a highway accident" and that this had involved a bullock cart. But could Kerouac's death have been merely accidental, as it was claimed?

In the interview at the panchayat headquarters they had been given a good many circumstantial facts, without conclusions. Unfortunately there had been no eyewitnesses on the road that day, which was normally well traveled.

From the details furnished, the two men were able to reconstruct what had happened—or what had probably happened—piecing the story together with their own assessment of the novelist's character and inclinations.

Kerouac was traveling by himself along the route leading from Dhabar Jat to Sawna when he came upon a cart pulled up at the side of the road with a lone driver. This struck him as strange because in Nghsi such a cart would usually have a crew to do the unloading.

The wagon was full of grain sacks. Kerouac struck up a conversation with the driver. The man appeared distraught and kept looking back at his load, which increased the novelist's suspicions.

Then it occurred to Kerouac that he had seen the man some months before at a wedding in Rampur. It had been in a courtyard with a canopy overhead. Around the fire the bride circled the prescribed seven times. In fact the man had been the bridegroom. The face of the child bride was unseen, and as she went around, hidden by the thick veil, Kerouac had noticed the man and been struck by his look of heavy sensuality. The man, who was middle-aged, had been somewhat drunk.

Somehow this look had increased Kerouac's own erotic feelings.

This was the fourteenth stage of the marriage cycle, in between the steps of Bida and Gaur. Therefore the man would already have spent some months living in the bride's house.

Now on the highway, the man did not want to talk with Kerouac and in fact lashed the bullock so it would go on.

Kerouac leaped on the back of the cart and began rummaging through the sacks. Sometime later he was found dead by people in a procession passing that way to market. The body had been crushed. It appeared that the cart had been driven over it.

Blake and the filmmaker discussed at some length this possible scenario. They had been present with Kerouac at the wedding, and had also noticed the behavior of the middle-aged bridegroom.

It occurred to them to wonder to what extent the death was unavoidable, or was simply the result of the novelist's curiosity.

The man was later apprehended for the murder of his wife. They had learned he had been on his way to dispose of the body, hidden under the grain sacks.

Only a week before this tragedy Kerouac had been sitting with Blake and Alvarez in the baithak, watching the pipe smoke coil as he listened to Blake's story.

It is unlikely that he had any premonition. And to what extent for the citizens of Altai, that is for the inhabitants of the country, was this death "real"?

The two remember him as he leaned against the post of the bunk, his head tangled in the mosquito netting.

BLAKE'S STORY CONTINUED: THE LIGHTS FESTIVAL

Egwegnu is the largest of the great Drune ecological universities. The period of study, initiated by what is called the "insect pilgrimage," lasts for six months. Tuition is subsidized by the confederacy, and couples come from all over the country of Nghsi-Altai. As the pilgrimage is made traditionally on the tenth year of marriage, the age range of the students is from about twenty-three to thirty years.

Again Venu and Sathan found themselves among people from the plains, and among city people as well. The couple was assigned to a point house. These combine dormitory apartments for the married students with laboratories and study rooms. The cluster of tall buildings of black metal and glass covered a promontory jutting out into the lake. Across the shine of water, they looked down on roofs of Egwegnu town obscured under dark trees.

Each apartment is equipped with a small kitchen where supper and breakfast are prepared. Or meals may be sent up by elevator from the dorm kitchen. The children of the students are taken care of by the cantonment, and are "adopted" by a Drune family during the day, returning to the apartment only in the evenings or on week ends.

Thus during this interval the young couples are free of cares, much as the university students in the West. No hard labor in the fields. No child-rearing duties. Solitude, quiet. The university means a break in the lives of these individual couples, a resting period and a relaxation from the pressures of tight communal living. As a matter of fact there is even a clinic in the dormitory where psychiatric counseling is offered to individuals suffering from the stresses of "overcommunalization." An interesting idea.

During the first months at Egwegnu students are required to take general courses. These, which are held in the open, are called Meditations and are the same for everyone. After that the student is expected to concentrate on some aspect of an environmental study having to do with his own geographic area.

The lecturers are the Deodars, the great "blue" shamans of Nghsi-Altai. It is said that they were the original people when the land was covered by forests, and that they invented the first musical and scientific instruments—in particular the sensor devices used in the weather and soils laboratories.

"Could you tell us what one of these meditations is like?" Alvarez had asked.

Blake gave the following account:

47

A LECTURE UNDER THE TREES

We are in a forest university, in a "lecture hall" under the trees listening to the famous Deodar lecturer, Totuola. An exceedingly tall man, with protruding shoulder blades. He is in his own flesh, the mark of priesthood.

The subject of this particular series of lectures has been "City Weather" and certain aspects of the recycling process. Totuola's talk is accompanied by slides. The slides, from a carousel or control console at the back behind the crowd, are projected simultaneously on ten screens hanging from the branches of trees.

Sun slants into the clearing. There is a slight rise toward the back (where the projector is located). The students sit at the lecturer's feet on the ground covered with pine needles.

The Deodar shows the slides. In one hand he holds a South Asian oboe which he uses as a pointer. From time to time—at the end of some difficult passage—he will blow on it, a long drawn-out dreamy single note, or several staccato jabs of varying pitches. This is to "dispel logical thought sequences" and "to concentrate the spirit" of the listener.

The following are some of Totuola's "thought sparks" (or koans) jotted down by one of the listeners at random.

1. Every breath out is heavier than the breath taken in. What is the exchange?

    •

2. The water cycle: Ocean ———→ to water vapor ———→ to windy rain ———→ to the rivulet feeding the Rampaging Red River.

    •

3. Don't ask the atom smasher to recycle life.

    •

4. If you want to comprehend the oyster you have to study salt water.

5. No individual without a commune.

●

6. The sovereign territory of Nghsi-Altai:
   4×10^{12} quanta Energy (solar radiation)/sq. ft./sec.
   The wealth of Nghsi-Altai:
   79.11% Nitrogen—20.96% Oxygen—.003% CO^2/cu. ft.
   of fresh air
   The frontiers of Nghsi-Altai:
   below 0° ice/above 100° steam

●

7. The holy man subjugates himself to the natural.

●

8. Learn to wind the clock before you take it apart.

●

9. Lake Erie died, January 1955—April 1968.

●

10. Man is not a geological force.

●

11. The soil cycle: Weathering of minerals ⟶ Tunneling
    of the earth by earth worms ⟶ Decay of butter-
    flies ⟶ men/giant lycopods (from the Mesozoic) ⟶
    Potassium and phosphorus deposits   At the end of
    each tiny root hair   colonies of nitrogen-fixing bacteria

●

12. The hawk is the scavenger.

●

13. The earth is 5 billion years old: inhabit it. Life is 1 billion
    years old: revere it. A strong sneeze will blow away 40,000
    years of topsoil.

●

14. The louse travels in the feathers of birds.

●

15. A good astronomer collects ants.

●

16. If you come on a one-dimensional system   look for decadence.

●

17. The carbon (breath) cycle:

$$6CO_2 + 5\ H_2 \xrightarrow[\text{animals}]{\text{plants (in the presence of light)}} C_6H_{10}O_5 + 6\ O_2$$

●

18. Four carbon bonds allow infinite complexity.

●

19. Go naked / walk with the leopard / carry a transistor radio.

●

20. Remake the prairie soil twice a century (lightning, fires, etc.).

●

21. The cell maintains an open steady state.
    The city maintains an open steady state.

●

22. If all the world were a supermarket   the study of limits   would be unnecessary.

●

23. A sweet soil is the result of many cataclysms.

●

24. The three great earth cycles: circulation of water/ formation of soil/ purification of air
The two great Festival Cycles: Savanni (dry) Sarhi (wet)

•

25. Gas penetrates / water dissolves / the membrane holds

•

26. Which of these two is the more complex:
an LCM (landing craft module)?
a milkweed pod?
i.e. has more operating parts?

•

27. The dry dandelion will float to the moon

•

28. Express all natural resources as constants, including the population constant.

•

29. It is dangerous to interfere with spontaneous arrangements

•

30. Power within nature: ecology
Power outside of nature: the shamans

"Those are beautiful," Kerouac had said. "And I see what you mean by the miraculous—as a quality of experience. Or of *possible* experience."

Alvarez asked: "What happened to our students? Did they graduate? Did Sathan and Venu return home?"

The story continued:

A week before graduation the two students were sitting in their guardian's study atop the Point House. Tattattatha, the young Deodar who had been assigned to them, was standing at the window. He was describing the coming Lights Festival. It would be celebrated on the lake at night. From the shore people would watch the "spirit boats."

The walls of the apartment were bare white without the woven prayer mandalas which one often finds in the cantonments. Here and there were sprigs of bamboo. A bunch of wheat stalks in a fired pot. The bright day, reflected from the surface of the lake, flooded through the open windows and made the white of the walls more intense.

The young tutor sat naked. In the light, the blue of his skin was intensified. An enormous thatch of kinky black hair crowned his face, in which a bow was tied. A leopard slept at his feet.

"So now you will go back to the old life," Tattattatha addressed them. "And I will go to the new." Their tutor would return to the plains with them to serve for the next year as the sensor at the Sawna Weather and Soils Station.

He asked them what they had learned during their "free" period.

Venu wondered whether they should not have come earlier, when they had been in their teens. Would it not have been better then? He felt his brain had been dulled by hard work and that he would have made a better student before the years of working as a cowherd and farmer, and before the cares of bringing up a family.

Sathan said, "We must obey the cycles."

Tattattatha sat at rest. The light wavered on the ceiling.

The guardian gazed at Venu.

"Wind Brother," he said, "your clan and phratry are guided by the weather. The atmosphere in all its aspects has been your study here. You have mastered the sky currents."

He turned to Sathan, whom he called "Moon Sister." "And your tribe's part among the Six Tendencies of Altai is mathematics and planning. So you have mastered cybernetics and have made a computer model of Venu's patch of sky. You have taken your insect wings together in this life phase."

"Now I must ask you: the sky and a region of the earth make a habitat, a biome. A biome is a living organism that exists within certain limits. Outside those it is dead, isn't that so?"

"Life is fragile."

"Well, ecology is the study of the web of life. And history, in a sense, is the study of breakdown—of the errors and diseases disintegrating the web. Civilizations have died of their mistakes. Now, would you say there is any such thing as a sentimental education?"

"No," Venu answered. "It has to be about truth."

"And the truth is, you have come here to be useful and good citizens. Not for individual development and expansion of consciousness. You have discovered your individuality. And with it an increased spirituality. But it's best not to overrate these things. Remember what the lecturer says: 'No individual without the commune.'"

"What do you mean, civilizations have died of their mistakes?" Sathan asked him.

"Through good, they have exceeded themselves and gone in the wrong direction. In the same way there are misdirections of love. During this Insect Pilgrimage, you have discovered sexual love; and you must not abuse it, but return it to the Commune. In the same way your studies must be directed back to the commune..."

That evening they went to the cantonment park. It was by the lake. Sathan and Venu strolled through it, along with many couples, walking arm in arm. On the benches under the lamplight a few of the students were reading books, and in the shadows couples embraced or laughed softly. Venu could feel the movement of Sathan's hips under her kurtah. On the lawn a quartet was playing Mozart. At the entrance to the park was a statue, an angel with a sword. On this was inscribed: "The Fruit of This Garden Is Forbidden. Taste It."

Inscribed on the opposite gate was: "Your Paradise Has Been Lost."

•　•

At the end of each term period there is what is called the Lights Festival. Students take samples of whatever they have been working on in the lab—leaves, grains, soils, etc.— plus strands of their own hair and photographs of themselves.

This is mixed with clay and formed into pots. Broken old pottery of former students, found on the shore, is also used. On the evening of the Lights Festival, these vessels are launched. When the moon rises, each couple places its boat on the lake, and floats it out, with a paper lantern burning in it. The lights drift out over the surface. And the children are allowed to throw stones at them and sink them. This is called: chrysalis-breaking. It is the end of the first life phase.

With the others at Egwegnu, Venu, Sathan, and the three children—Srikant, Maddi, and Dhillon—did this, participating in the rites. The next day they left the Drune cantonment for Sawna, their native village, accompanied by the young sensor.

END OF BOOK I

Arrival is the first book of the tetralogy DAILY LIVES IN
NGHSI-ALTAI.

    I. *Arrival*
   II. *Gahr City*
  III. *Harditts in Sawna*
  IV. *Exile*

The first two books have been scheduled for publication,
respectively, for fall 1977 and spring 1978 by New Directions.
The final volumes will appear in the near future.

Red Shift: An Introduction to Nghsi-Altai has been published
by Penny Each Press, Thetford, Vermont 05074.